How to Draw
Goosebumps®

WRITTEN AND ILLUSTRATED BY RON ZALME

ISBN   978-0-545-24895-2

Goosebumps book series created by Parachute Press, Inc.
Copyright © 2010 by Scholastic Inc.

12 11 10 9 8 7 6 5 4 3 2 1   10 11 12 13 14 15/0

Designed by Steve Scott
Printed in the U.S.A.   40
First printing, September 2010

SCHOLASTIC INC.

NEW YORK   TORONTO   LONDON   AUCKLAND   SYDNEY   MEXICO CITY   NEW DELHI   HONG KONG

DRAWING CAN BE A . . . *SCREAM!*

The Goosebumps creatures are after you! Your only hope is to get to them first . . . on paper! Follow the steps ahead, one by one, and you will learn how to capture and tame the things that give you . . . **Goosebumps!**

CREATURE-CAPTURING EQUIPMENT

PENCIL: A basic #2 pencil will suit most of your drawing needs.

PAPER: Printer paper or tracing paper is a great way to warm up.

ERASER: A soft eraser that doesn't smudge easily and has edges to get into those tight spots is best.

RULERS, CIRCLE GUIDES, ELLIPSE GUIDES, AND SHAPED CURVES: These can add a smooth finished look to your drawing.

COLOR: Pens, markers, colored pencils, watercolors, or paints can be used together or separately.

STEPS ARE GETTING CLOSER . . .

The steps to a horrifically good drawing are just a page away! Each featured *Goosebumps* character has been reduced to a series of simple shapes and lines so you can learn how to build your drawing. Each lesson begins with a series of action lines (drawn in black) to help you pose the character and capture its attitude, followed by some simple shapes (drawn in blue) to guide you through creating a framework over which you will construct your finished drawing. Each additional step will add form and detail until your drawing is complete.

Once the sketch is done, your job will be to clean and refine your artwork. Use your eraser to wipe away your foundation lines and then darken the line work that best defines your creepy *Goosebumps* character! The last step shows the character without the sketch lines so you can compare your work to the original.

After that, you decide how far you would like to express yourself artistically. Add color, use imaginative materials, anything that comes to mind to bring your drawing to life . . . or death, whichever suits the creature you've created.

SHAPE-SHIFTING

While you are drawing with pencil on paper, you are working with flat *two-dimensional* shapes: circles, ovals, squares, rectangles, and triangles.

But an artist must **shift** his or her way of thinking to imagine *flat*-drawn shapes in terms of *three-dimensional* shapes. This 3-D frame of mind helps to create an *illusion* of depth and volume in the drawing and will help to make your artwork look more real and exciting. The 3-D forms you will use are: spheres, cubes, cylinders, cones, and pyramids.

DON'T BE SCARED!

The real secret to **ALL** drawing is building every illustration, like a series of layers, from simple basic shapes to a final piece of artwork. No one will see all the construction steps you worked through to get to your finished piece.

You're all set to get started! Just remember: Drawing takes practice, so don't be discouraged if you don't get the results you expect right away. Keep at it, and your confidence in your abilities will grow—and your talent may surprise you. It may even give you . . . ***Goosebumps!***

NIGHT OF THE LIVING DUMMY

He's alive! Alive . . . With his painted grin and beat up bow tie, Slappy looks like an ordinary ventriloquist's dummy. But this troublemaking block of wood is anything but dumb. Slappy the living dummy is a walking, stalking, trash-talking terror. And behind that big, bad, blinking exterior is an icy heart.

1 Begin your first sketch with two arching action lines (shown in black). Using these lines as a guide, carefully position the large oval (shown in blue) for Slappy's head. Always pay careful attention to your proportions and positioning. Note that where the action lines meet is lower than the center of the oval. Add the horizontal features line and finish with the bow tie shape at the bottom.

DRAWING TIP ALWAYS SKETCH LIGHTLY. BUILD THE DRAWING SLOWLY AND DARKEN YOUR LINES AS YOU BECOME CERTAIN YOU HAVE DRAWN THEM CORRECTLY. THE UNWANTED LINES WILL BE MUCH EASIER TO ERASE THAT WAY.

2 Within the large oval, sketch in the smaller skull-like shape of Slappy's head. The right and left sides are basically a mirror image of each other. Next, place the eyebrows and nose over your guides using the features line to help you position them correctly. Finish the step by adding the mouth and hairline.

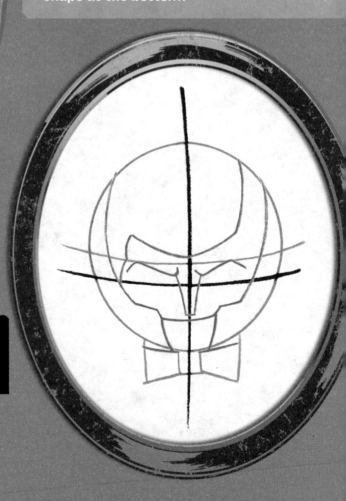

3

Now that most of your large foundation shapes have been placed, you can begin to add detail to define your character. Start with the scary glare of Slappy's eyes and then finish his nose and mouth. Add an ear to each side of the head and finish off the details for the hair and bow tie. Do you see how Slappy is forming? Almost done!

4

Add a few last details like hair and freckles, and your drawing is complete. Time to clean it up! Using your eraser, carefully remove all of your unwanted construction lines and darken the lines that best capture Slappy's evil nature. Notice how some of the lines around Slappy's face are thicker. Varying the thickness of your line work makes for a more lively drawing. But is that a good thing for an evil dummy? You decide!

FEAR FACT: *SLAPPY CAN BE BROUGHT TO LIFE AND PUT TO SLEEP BY SAYING, "KARRU MARRI ODONNA LOMA MOLONU KARRANO," WHICH MEANS, "YOU AND I ARE ONE NOW."*

THE HAUNTED MASK

You've got the look . . . What goes on must come off. Unless, of course, you're talking about the Haunted Mask! Although the latex face pulls on easily enough, it has a bad habit of sticking. To your skin. Forever. Unless you can figure out how to get it off. Yeah, right. Good luck!

1

Begin your first sketch with the two cros arching lines—notice the lean to the righ and the gentle curve of the horizontal Once more, proceed to add the large hea circle, shifted slightly to the left of center Draw a smaller circle below the first and joi them with simple jaw lines as shown. Don' forget the horizontal features line!

DRAWING TIP LIGHTING IS IMPORTANT AND CAN MAKE YOUR DRAWING DRAMATIC OR SCARY. HAVE YOU EVER HELD A FLASHLIGHT UNDER YOUR CHIN AT NIGHT? SPOOKY, RIGHT? TRY SHADING ONE OF YOUR DRAWINGS THAT WAY.

2

Draw the two eyes first; the one on the right is just a bit larger than the one on the left. Then draw the semicircle for the top of the head. If you draw the cheekbones next, it will help you to locate and place the large pointy ears. Finish the step by drawing the large mouth and then squaring off the chin.

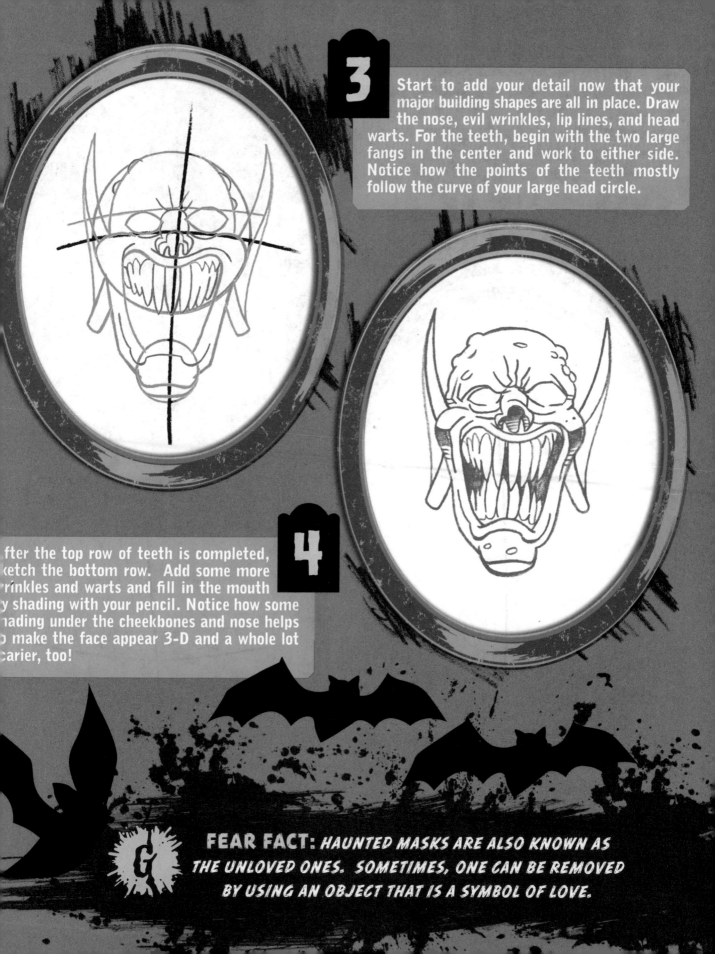

3 Start to add your detail now that your major building shapes are all in place. Draw the nose, evil wrinkles, lip lines, and head warts. For the teeth, begin with the two large fangs in the center and work to either side. Notice how the points of the teeth mostly follow the curve of your large head circle.

4 fter the top row of teeth is completed, ketch the bottom row. Add some more rinkles and warts and fill in the mouth y shading with your pencil. Notice how some hading under the cheekbones and nose helps make the face appear 3-D and a whole lot carier, too!

FEAR FACT: *HAUNTED MASKS ARE ALSO KNOWN AS THE UNLOVED ONES. SOMETIMES, ONE CAN BE REMOVED BY USING AN OBJECT THAT IS A SYMBOL OF LOVE.*

HOW I GOT MY SHRUNKEN HEAD

With his leather face and stitched-up lips this bad boy is heads and pony-tail better than other monsters in the jungle. Even though Shrunken Heads are a bunch of no-bodies, they know how to stay a-head of the game. But just take a deep look into their hollow eyes and you might need to get your head examined. . . .

1 Make a cross of action lines and then add the large head circle, but this time the circle is centered. Make two light feature-placement lines—one for the eyes and one for the mouth. Draw a small oval underneath the large circle.

2 Position the eyes between the horizontal guides as shown. Next, draw the semicircle for the top of the head, evenly spaced within your first circle. Take note of the difference between the jaw lines on the two sides of the face and draw them. Add the nose, some stitches along the mouth line, and finish by connecting the lower oval to the head with lines that mimic hair.

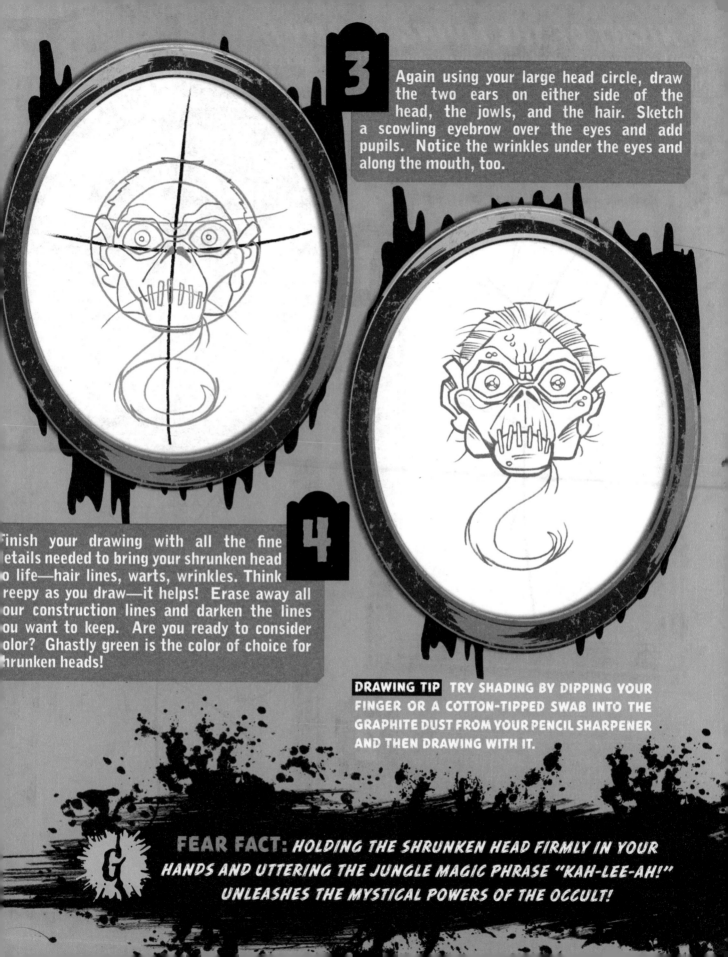

3

Again using your large head circle, draw the two ears on either side of the head, the jowls, and the hair. Sketch a scowling eyebrow over the eyes and add pupils. Notice the wrinkles under the eyes and along the mouth, too.

4

Finish your drawing with all the fine details needed to bring your shrunken head to life—hair lines, warts, wrinkles. Think creepy as you draw—it helps! Erase away all your construction lines and darken the lines you want to keep. Are you ready to consider color? Ghastly green is the color of choice for shrunken heads!

DRAWING TIP TRY SHADING BY DIPPING YOUR FINGER OR A COTTON-TIPPED SWAB INTO THE GRAPHITE DUST FROM YOUR PENCIL SHARPENER AND THEN DRAWING WITH IT.

FEAR FACT: *HOLDING THE SHRUNKEN HEAD FIRMLY IN YOUR HANDS AND UTTERING THE JUNGLE MAGIC PHRASE "KAH-LEE-AH!" UNLEASHES THE MYSTICAL POWERS OF THE OCCULT!*

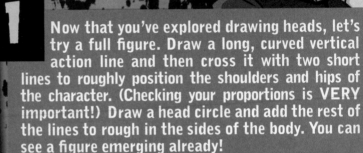

Amy had a perfectly good ventriloquist's dummy, Dennis, except that his head kept falling off. So she got a new one from a pawn shop—Slappy. Big mistake. At first, it's almost magical how Slappy can seem to read her mind, and her comedy routine starts to really shine—until Slappy starts a routine of his own! A routine designed to enslave Amy!

1

Now that you've explored drawing heads, let's try a full figure. Draw a long, curved vertical action line and then cross it with two short lines to roughly position the shoulders and hips of the character. (Checking your proportions is VERY important!) Draw a head circle and add the rest of the lines to rough in the sides of the body. You can see a figure emerging already!

2

Much like you did for Slappy's head shot, add the eyes and face sides using your guidelines to help place them correctly. Now move on to add the shapes that will become Slappy's jacket, arms, and trousers. Follow the diagram. A few simple angled lines are enough to block in the shapes for his shoes.

3 After all the foundation shapes have been plotted, you can begin to add the details to define the look of the character. Study the example for a moment and then proceed to draw Slappy's ears, nose, and hairline. Then draw his jacket lapels, buttons, and hands. Finally, complete his shoes.

DRAWING TIP ANIMATORS LIKE TO SKETCH IN BLUE PENCIL TO KEEP THEIR SKETCH LINES LIGHT, SIMILAR TO THE WAY THESE STEPS ARE DONE.

4 Refine your drawing. Do your usual cleanup with the eraser and then darken the lines that most look like Slappy. Add the remaining details: hair, freckles, clothing folds, etc. Thickening the outline in places can add some flair and style to your drawing. And, of course, the fun of adding color speaks for itself . . . just like Slappy!

FEAR FACT: *SOME PEOPLE BELIEVE THAT SLAPPY HAS THE POWER TO CONTROL PEOPLE'S MINDS AND TURN PEOPLE INTO PUPPETS.*

Carly Beth was lucky—she eventually managed to get the living haunted mask to peel from her face. Steve Boswell, the jealous prankster who had tormented her, wanted a Halloween costume scarier than hers, so he acquired a mask, too. He wasn't as lucky. He began cackling like a cranky old maniac the minute he put it on. The mask had possessed him to carry out its own evil plans!

1

Each of the action lines is gently curved. Lightly sketch all three. Draw in the head circle with a features line and jaw lines. See how the head forms just as it did for the face lesson you did earlier? Draw a base line lower down on the vertical action line so you get a sense of your proportions and then complete the basic shapes for the body and leg.

2

Sketch in some of the basic facial features: eyes, nose, and mouth. Then block in the simple shapes as shown to complete the figure: arms, hands, legs, and feet. Notice that the leg on the right is somewhat larger than the one on the left and appears to come forward. This is a spatial technique used by artists called foreshortening.

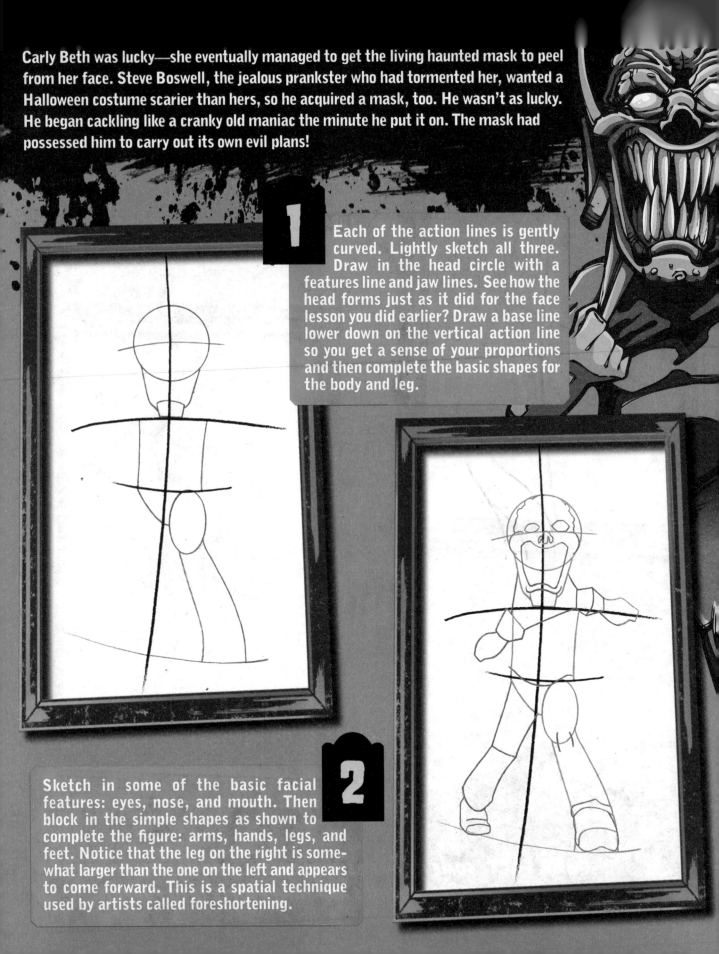

3 Your basic construction is done. Time to add all the frightening details! As you did with the head lesson, add the ears, eyebrows, and teeth. Draw in the fingers and the lines that radiate from them to show that the mask is stretchy. A few clothing wrinkles and shoelaces and you're ready to go to finish!

DRAWING TIP A MEDIUM IS AN ARTIST'S MATERIAL OR SPECIFIC TECHNIQUE. A MEDIUM IS ALSO A PERSON WHO ACTS AS A LIVING LINK TO THOSE IN THE SUPERNATURAL WORLD. COINCIDENCE?

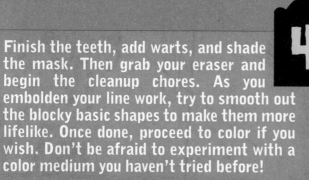

4 Finish the teeth, add warts, and shade the mask. Then grab your eraser and begin the cleanup chores. As you embolden your line work, try to smooth out the blocky basic shapes to make them more lifelike. Once done, proceed to color if you wish. Don't be afraid to experiment with a color medium you haven't tried before!

FEAR FACT: *FINDING A "SYMBOL OF LOVE" DIDN'T REMOVE THE MASK FROM STEVE'S FACE THE WAY IT DID FOR CARLY BETH. EACH MASK SEEMS TO HAVE ITS OWN SPECIAL "KEY" FOR REMOVAL . . . IF YOU CAN FIND IT IN TIME!*

THE MASTER OF SCAREMONIES

Boo, Dude! . . . Introducing the Master of Scaremonies, the bones behind the business, the guy everyone digs . . . up! Curly loves to rib his very best buds with very bad jokes, like: "Did you hear the one about the corpse? I died when I heard it!" No bones about it: You'll bust a gut (or crack a rib) laughing way too hard with the Curl-meister. So next time you're digging around for freaky, shrieky fun, contact the ghost host with the most.

1 Use your ruler and draw the long vertical action line at a slant. This will help you to achieve the proper stance for Curly. Draw the two horizontals and begin to rough in the basic shapes. Start with the head, and it will be easier to place the arms and hands. Add the kneecap (basically a modified oval) and finish with the rectangle for the foot.

2 Add a hairline, eyes, mouth, and glasses to the head circle you sketched. Then align Curly's kerchief over the top horizontal action line. Connect Curly's hip to his kneecap, then his kneecap to his foot with bones as shown. Then rough in the other leg and foot.

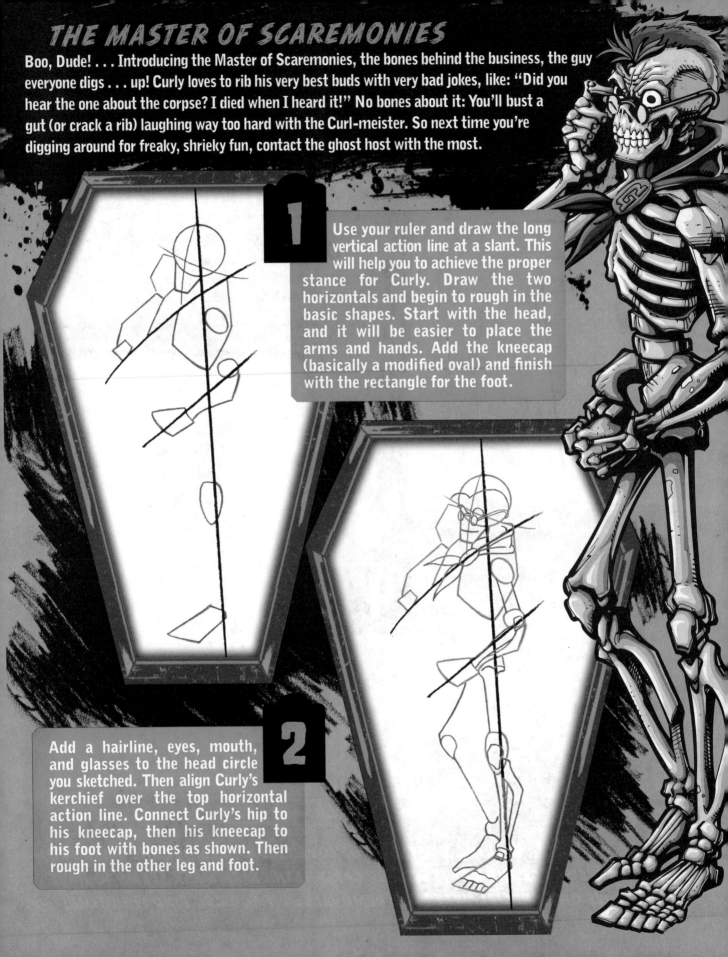

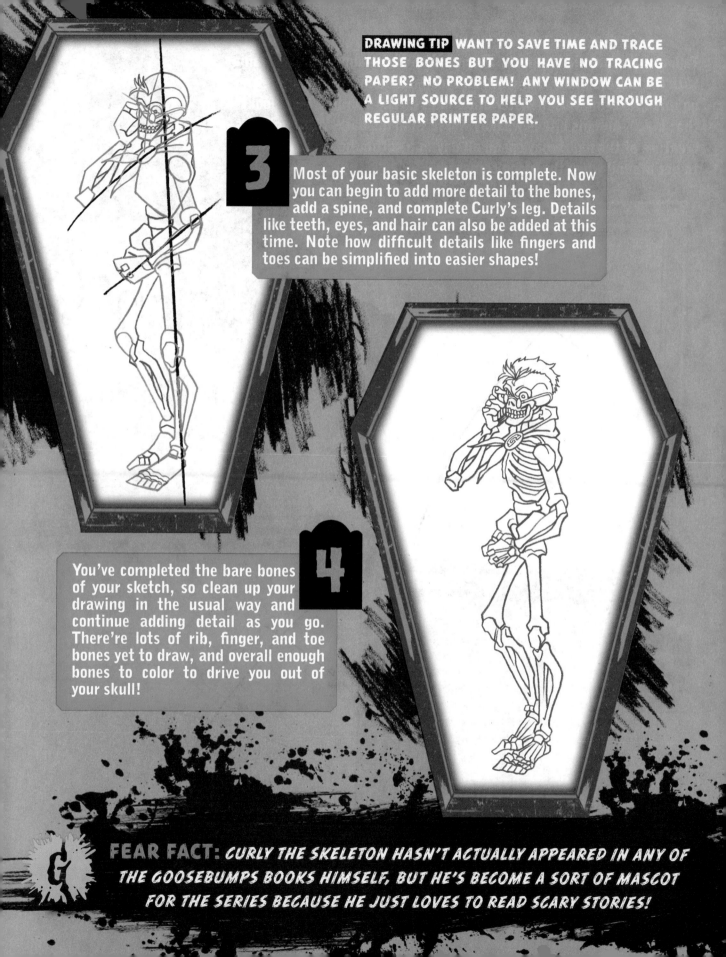

DRAWING TIP WANT TO SAVE TIME AND TRACE THOSE BONES BUT YOU HAVE NO TRACING PAPER? NO PROBLEM! ANY WINDOW CAN BE A LIGHT SOURCE TO HELP YOU SEE THROUGH REGULAR PRINTER PAPER.

3 Most of your basic skeleton is complete. Now you can begin to add more detail to the bones, add a spine, and complete Curly's leg. Details like teeth, eyes, and hair can also be added at this time. Note how difficult details like fingers and toes can be simplified into easier shapes!

4 You've completed the bare bones of your sketch, so clean up your drawing in the usual way and continue adding detail as you go. There're lots of rib, finger, and toe bones yet to draw, and overall enough bones to color to drive you out of your skull!

FEAR FACT: CURLY THE SKELETON HASN'T ACTUALLY APPEARED IN ANY OF THE GOOSEBUMPS BOOKS HIMSELF, BUT HE'S BECOME A SORT OF MASCOT FOR THE SERIES BECAUSE HE JUST LOVES TO READ SCARY STORIES!

VAMPIRE BREATH

Talk about a pain in the neck...Born in the mountains of Transylvania with his morbid pallor, dark-ringed eyes, and bloody fangs, there's no mis-stake-ing this monster of darkness. The Vampire has "looks that kill." And his bite is waaaay worse than his bark. Although this creature of the night may spend all day in a coffin, he sure knows how to get around when the moon comes up.

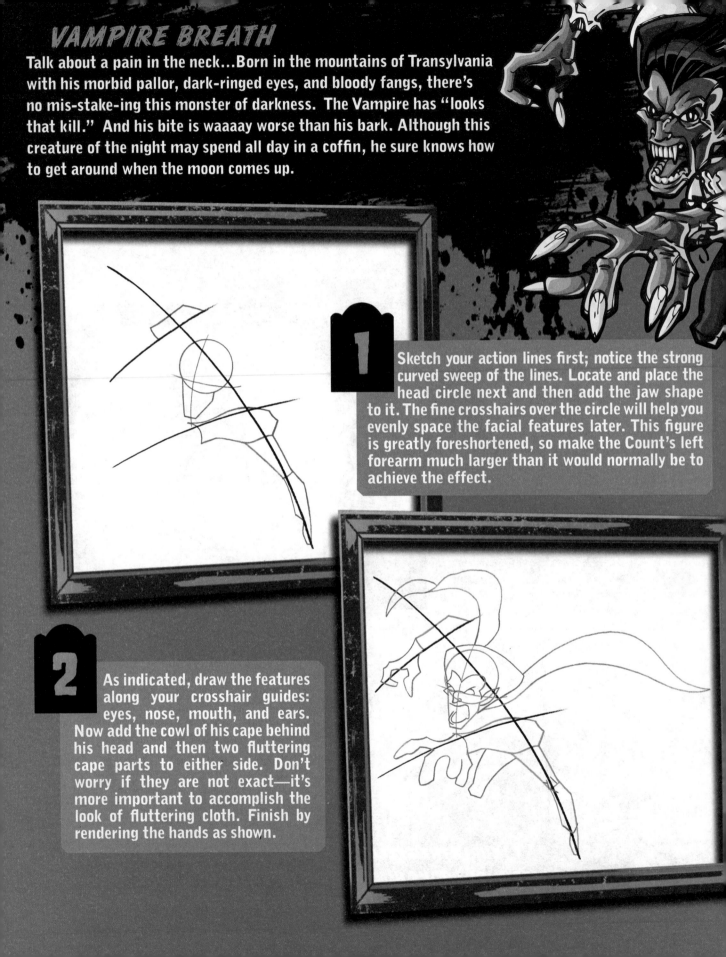

1 Sketch your action lines first; notice the strong curved sweep of the lines. Locate and place the head circle next and then add the jaw shape to it. The fine crosshairs over the circle will help you evenly space the facial features later. This figure is greatly foreshortened, so make the Count's left forearm much larger than it would normally be to achieve the effect.

2 As indicated, draw the features along your crosshair guides: eyes, nose, mouth, and ears. Now add the cowl of his cape behind his head and then two fluttering cape parts to either side. Don't worry if they are not exact—it's more important to accomplish the look of fluttering cloth. Finish by rendering the hands as shown.

3 Now that most of your foundation is in place, begin adding detail over your framework: fingernails, clothing and cape, eyes, teeth, and fangs. (It's very important to have fangs!) Complete the Count's other leg, and you're ready to proceed!

DRAWING TIP TIE A LIGHT THREAD OR STRING TO YOUR PENCIL NEAR THE TIP AND THEN PIN IT TO YOUR PAPER WITH A THUMBTACK. KEEP THE STRING TIGHT AS YOU MOVE YOUR PENCIL IN A CIRCLE AROUND THE TACK. INSTANT COMPASS!

4 Sketch the hair as shown, and have fun shading and drawing the finer details such as knuckles, wrinkles, and teeth. Follow the usual erasing routine and liven up your artwork with some color. It's been a while since the Count was lively . . . he'll appreciate it!

FEAR FACT: *ALL VAMPIRES HAVE THEIR OWN UNIQUE BOTTLE OF VAMPIRE'S BREATH, WHICH GIVES THEM THE MAGICAL ABILITY TO TIME TRAVEL!*

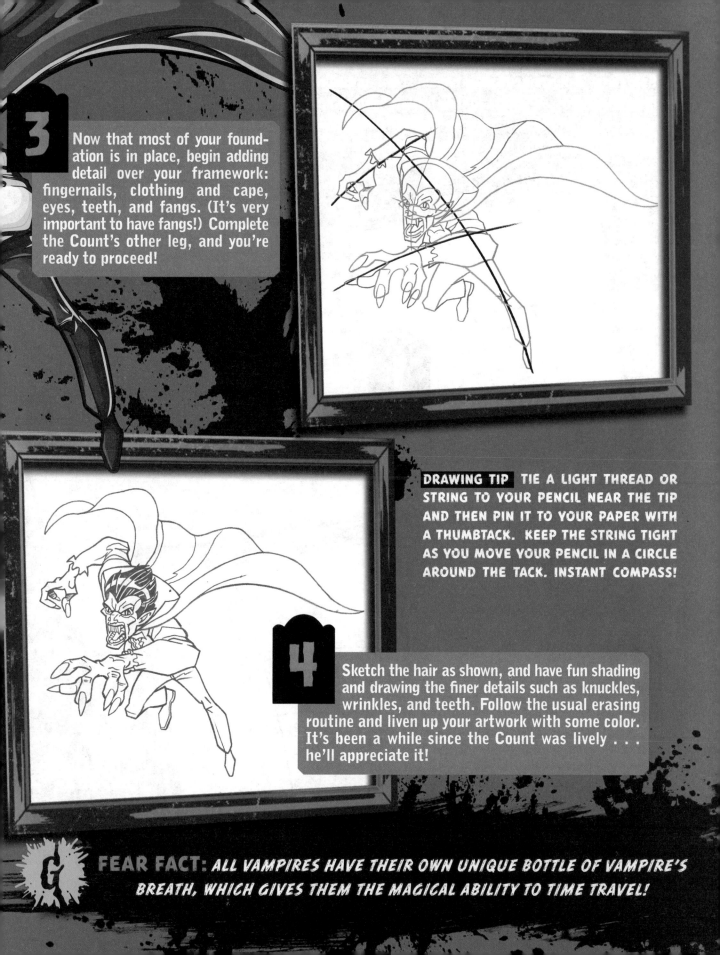

THE SCARECROW WALKS AT MIDNIGHT

Welcome to my field of screams! . . . Meet a straw-stuffed monster which really is for the birds! This Scarecrow's permanent, painted-on scowl and cold, black, beady eyes would give anyone the shivers. All dressed up in raggedy burlap, ripped-up clothes, and a fearfully floppy hat, he's heard all about big hoedowns on the farm. And now he's the one who's getting down . . . off his pole! It's time for the sack of straw to come alive in the cornfields and beyond. . . .

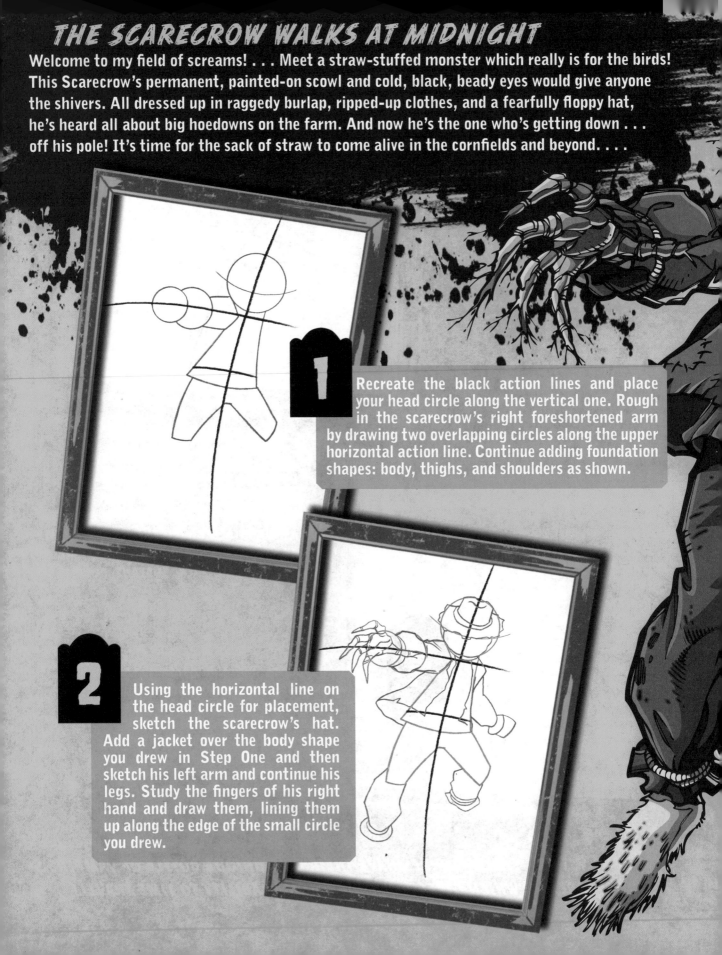

1 Recreate the black action lines and place your head circle along the vertical one. Rough in the scarecrow's right foreshortened arm by drawing two overlapping circles along the upper horizontal action line. Continue adding foundation shapes: body, thighs, and shoulders as shown.

2 Using the horizontal line on the head circle for placement, sketch the scarecrow's hat. Add a jacket over the body shape you drew in Step One and then sketch his left arm and continue his legs. Study the fingers of his right hand and draw them, lining them up along the edge of the small circle you drew.

3 Time to begin to focus on the detail! Draw the eyes and stitched mouth and the ropes that bind his neck, wrists, and ankles. Give him a belt, too. Now complete the figure by drawing the feet and pitchfork.

DRAWING TIP WANT A NEAT TRICK TO ADD TEXTURE? PLACE A ROUGH-TEXTURED FABRIC LIKE BURLAP OR ROUGH SANDPAPER BEHIND YOUR DRAWING AND SHADE WITH THE SIDE OF YOUR PENCIL. THE PENCIL WILL REPRODUCE THE TEXTURE INTO YOUR DRAWING! WHAT OTHER MATERIALS DO YOU THINK WILL WORK?

4 Lots of scary detail can be added to make your scarecrow creepy! Render his straw feet, add roots to his hat and fingers, and cover his outfit with dirt and grime. (Hint: It might be easier for you if you do the erasing before adding all the little final touches. If you've finished drawing your scarecrow correctly, it'll be more than just crows he'll be scaring!)

FEAR FACT: STANLEY THE FARMHAND SEEMS TO HOLD THE SECRET OF THE SCARECROWS WITHIN HIS BOOK OF SUPERSTITIONS. WHAT ELSE IS HE HIDING?

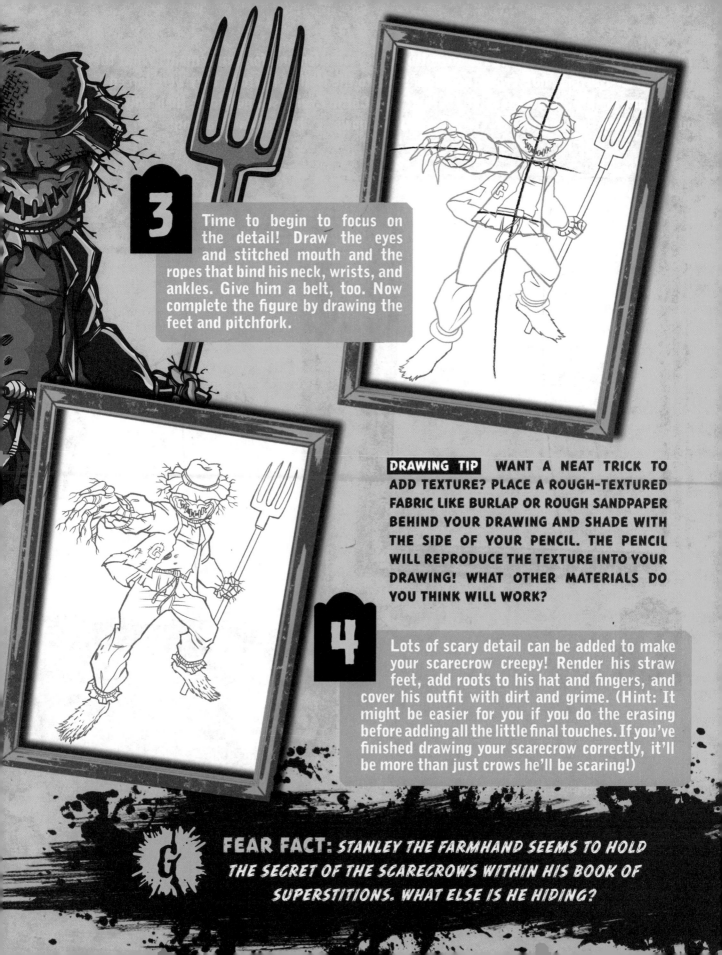

The Morris family was looking for adventure. They were looking for amusement. What they found was—HorrorLand! From the Doom Slide to the Hall of Mirrors, they were forced to ride one deadly attraction after another! The Coffin Cruise seemed to be their only way out, but could they survive it? The Ticket Taker knows . . . but he's not talking!

1 Reproduce the usual action lines as shown and align the head circle. Don't forget the crosshairs for the features! Once again, we're dealing with a greatly foreshortened arm, so sketch your basic shapes for the Ticket Taker's right arm fairly large. Now, using your guides for placement, add the right leg.

2 Carefully draw the Ticket Taker's features—eyes, nose, and mouth—along the crosshair guides, then add the points of his horns as shown. (We'll add the rest later.) Create the belly and belt line and rough in the shapes for his left leg. Now you can convert the stiff lines of his arm into muscular shapes. Pay attention to how lines overlap to keep the illusion of the hand being forward of the body.

3 Add eyebrow ridges, fangs, and two more sections of his horns. Move on to add more muscle to his foreshortened arm. Sketch in the circle for his roll of tickets and connect it to his body with a thick arm. Add his feet and some preliminary wrinkle lines.

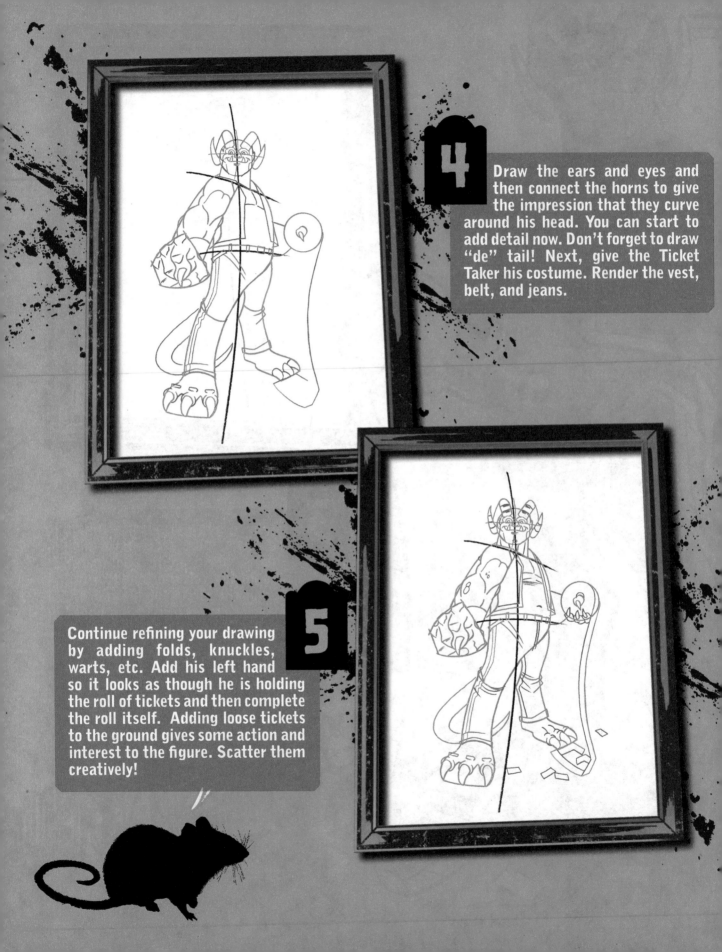

4

Draw the ears and eyes and then connect the horns to give the impression that they curve around his head. You can start to add detail now. Don't forget to draw "de" tail! Next, give the Ticket Taker his costume. Render the vest, belt, and jeans.

5

Continue refining your drawing by adding folds, knuckles, warts, etc. Add his left hand so it looks as though he is holding the roll of tickets and then complete the roll itself. Adding loose tickets to the ground gives some action and interest to the figure. Scatter them creatively!

6

Finish with your normal cleaning and erasing and then look for ways to add more realism and scariness to your drawing. Darken some of the lines and add texture and shadows to make the figure more dramatic. You've been working so hard at this you're probably ready for a vacation! We understand that HorrorLand has plenty of free parking.

DRAWING TIP IF YOU DON'T HAVE A COMPASS OR CIRCLE GUIDE HANDY, TRY USING REGULAR HOUSEHOLD ITEMS TO MAKE PERFECT CIRCLES. TRACING AROUND BUTTONS AND COINS IS GREAT FOR SMALL CIRCLES. JARS, CANS, AND BOWLS ARE TERRIFIC FOR LARGE ONES.

FEAR FACT: *LIZZIE MORRIS THOUGHT IT ODD THAT THE PARK SHOULD HAVE SO MANY SIGNS WARNING AGAINST PINCHING. COULD THAT BE A CLUE LEADING TO ESCAPE?*

Bite on . . . One thing's fur sure: The Werewolf needs a monster makeover. This beast's covered from hea to toe in a nasty, matted pelt. His teeth are pointy like spears. His claws are jagged-edged. Worst of al He's a drooling fool! And don't even mention his glowing eyes. The Werewolf is cursed with beastly bad looks. Someone buy this were-guy a flea collar! He's all dressed up with no place to howl!

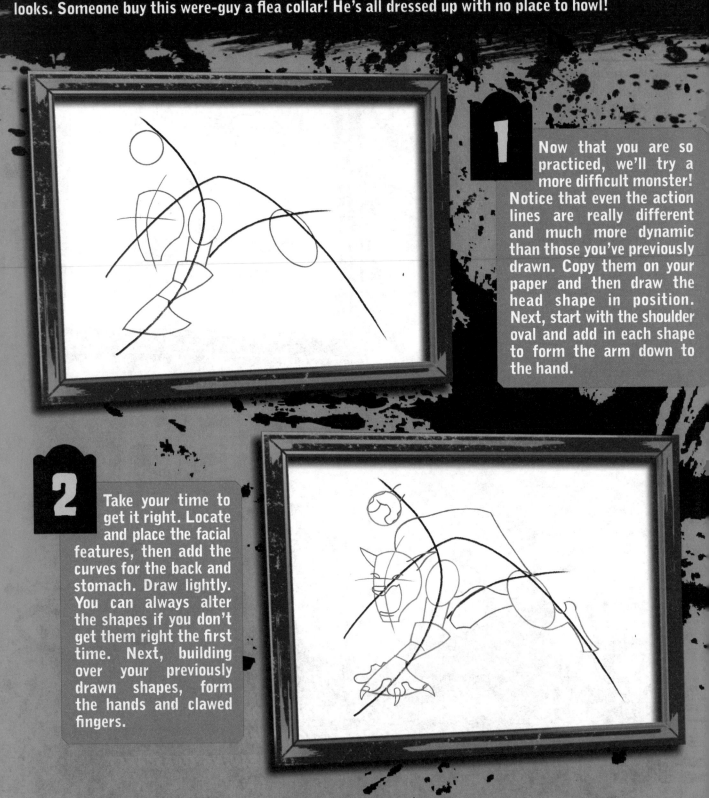

1 Now that you are so practiced, we'll try a more difficult monster! Notice that even the action lines are really different and much more dynamic than those you've previously drawn. Copy them on your paper and then draw the head shape in position. Next, start with the shoulder oval and add in each shape to form the arm down to the hand.

2 Take your time to get it right. Locate and place the facial features, then add the curves for the back and stomach. Draw lightly. You can always alter the shapes if you don't get them right the first time. Next, building over your previously drawn shapes, form the hands and clawed fingers.

3 Add the last of the basic shapes like hind legs, raised arm, and tail. Now you can start altering your rigid geometric shapes to look like fur. Think hairy and convert your previous line work to werewolf fur, but not all of it! Vary the line and size of your fur clumps.

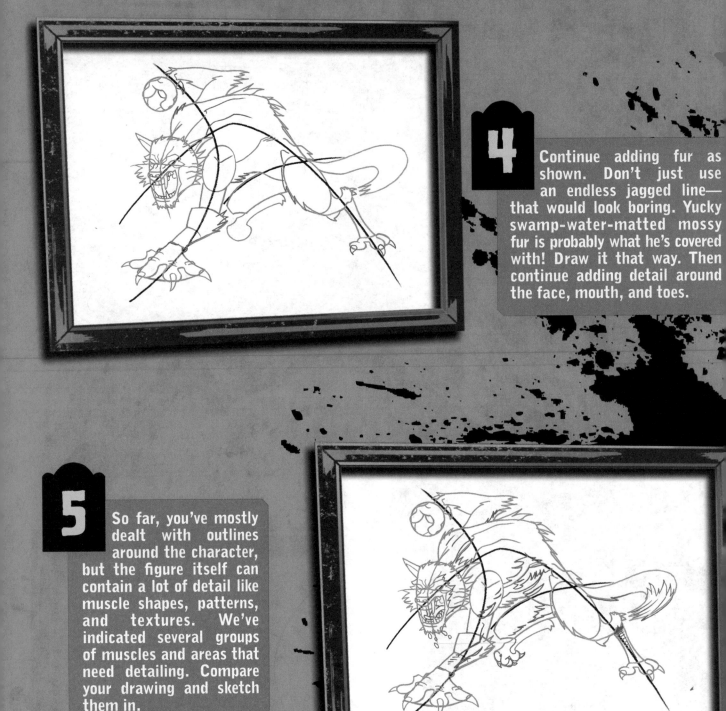

4 Continue adding fur as shown. Don't just use an endless jagged line— that would look boring. Yucky swamp-water-matted mossy fur is probably what he's covered with! Draw it that way. Then continue adding detail around the face, mouth, and toes.

5 So far, you've mostly dealt with outlines around the character, but the figure itself can contain a lot of detail like muscle shapes, patterns, and textures. We've indicated several groups of muscles and areas that need detailing. Compare your drawing and sketch them in.

DRAWING TIP A PIECE OF BENDABLE WIRE CAN MAKE A GREAT DRAWING AID. JUST BEND IT TO THE DESIRED SHAPE AND DRAW ALONG IT TO MAKE A SMOOTHLY DRAWN CURVE.

6 Compare your drawing to the example. Did you get it right? It's a tough one! Make adjustments if you need to and then clean up with your eraser and go to finish. Shade for the fear effect and consider color. Being artistic means lots of hard work and effort.

FEAR FACT: *A HUNDRED YEARS PRIOR TO GRADY'S WEREWOLF TROUBLES, EVERYONE IN THE NEARBY TOWN CAUGHT SOMETHING FROM THE SWAMP THAT STARTED WITH A FEVER. MOST DIED, BUT THOSE WHO DIDN'T WENT CRAZY.*

Mummy's the word . . . Ancient Egypt. Pyramids. Camels. And an amazing, well preserved mummy — all wrapped up with nowhere to go. Until now! Prince Khor-Ru has seen lurking deep within ancient Egyptian tunnels and tombs for more than four thousand years. But now he's awake again, back from the afterlife. The embalming fluid's all dried up. The scarabs have left the building. And he wants to dust himself off and get busy. All the Prince needs now is a helping hand from you!

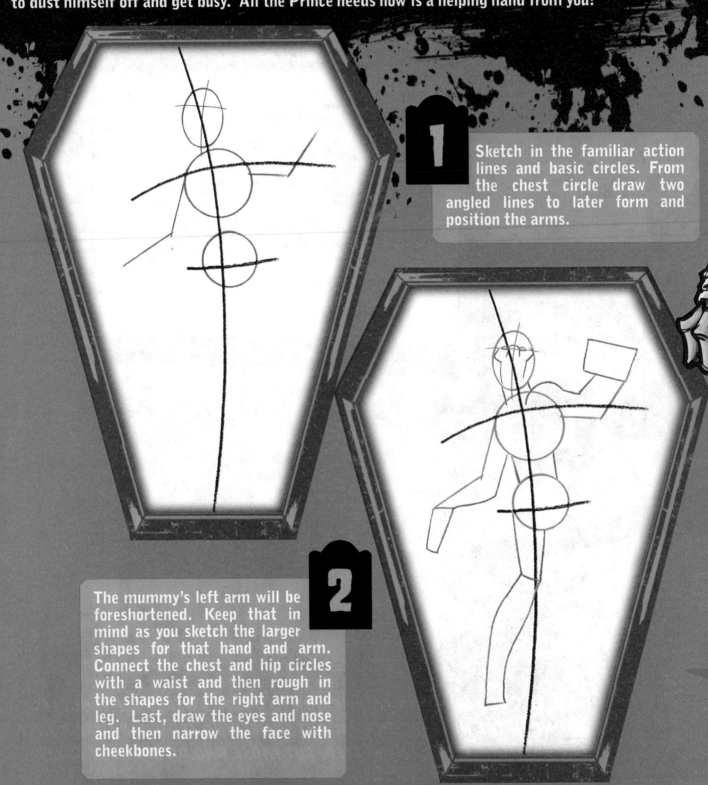

1 Sketch in the familiar action lines and basic circles. From the chest circle draw two angled lines to later form and position the arms.

2 The mummy's left arm will be foreshortened. Keep that in mind as you sketch the larger shapes for that hand and arm. Connect the chest and hip circles with a waist and then rough in the shapes for the right arm and leg. Last, draw the eyes and nose and then narrow the face with cheekbones.

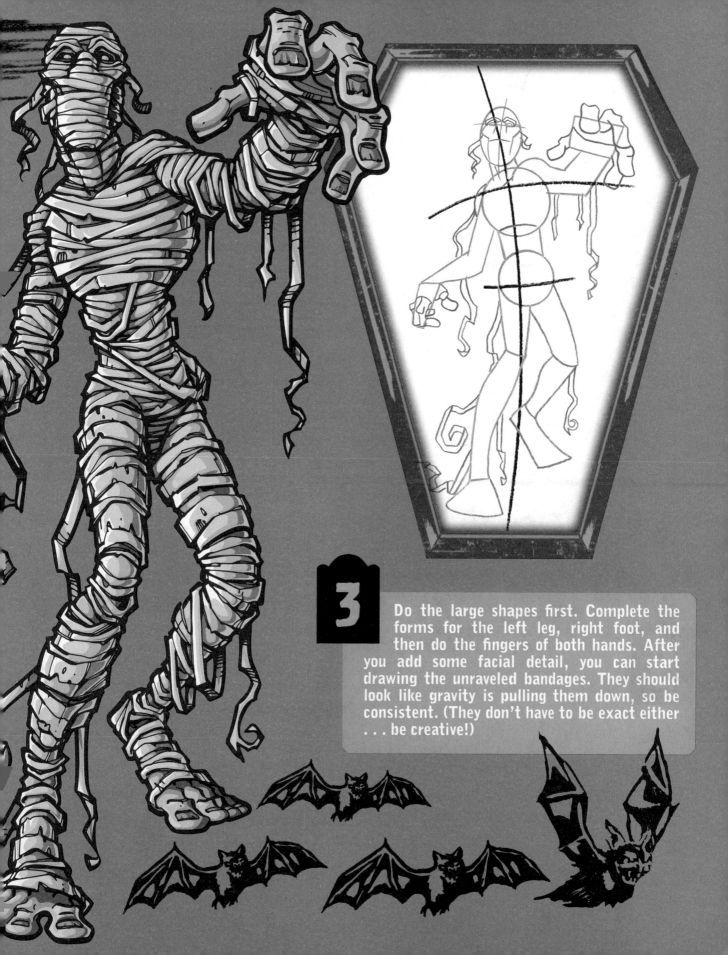

3

Do the large shapes first. Complete the forms for the left leg, right foot, and then do the fingers of both hands. After you add some facial detail, you can start drawing the unraveled bandages. They should look like gravity is pulling them down, so be consistent. (They don't have to be exact either . . . be creative!)

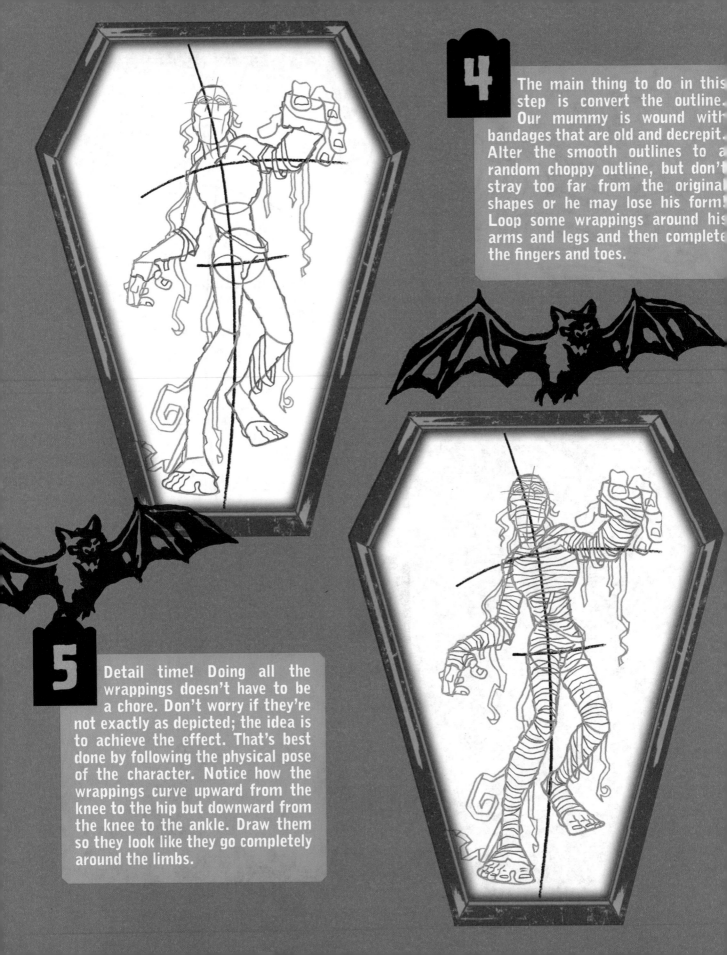

The main thing to do in this step is convert the outline. Our mummy is wound with bandages that are old and decrepit. Alter the smooth outlines to a random choppy outline, but don't stray too far from the original shapes or he may lose his form! Loop some wrappings around his arms and legs and then complete the fingers and toes.

5

Detail time! Doing all the wrappings doesn't have to be a chore. Don't worry if they're not exactly as depicted; the idea is to achieve the effect. That's best done by following the physical pose of the character. Notice how the wrappings curve upward from the knee to the hip but downward from the knee to the ankle. Draw them so they look like they go completely around the limbs.

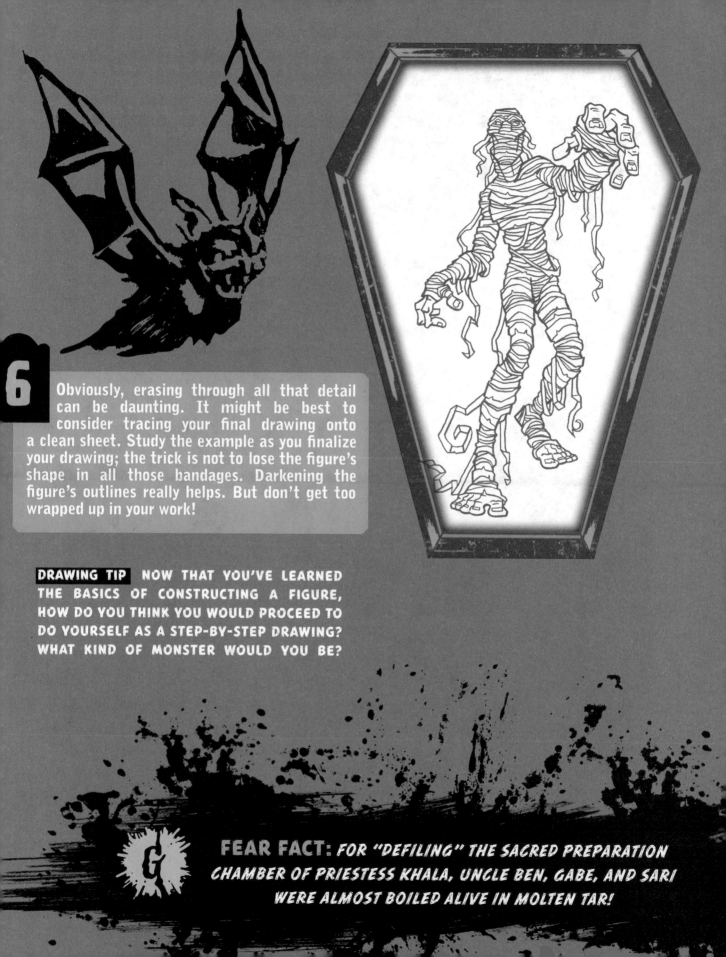

6 Obviously, erasing through all that detail can be daunting. It might be best to consider tracing your final drawing onto a clean sheet. Study the example as you finalize your drawing; the trick is not to lose the figure's shape in all those bandages. Darkening the figure's outlines really helps. But don't get too wrapped up in your work!

DRAWING TIP NOW THAT YOU'VE LEARNED THE BASICS OF CONSTRUCTING A FIGURE, HOW DO YOU THINK YOU WOULD PROCEED TO DO YOURSELF AS A STEP-BY-STEP DRAWING? WHAT KIND OF MONSTER WOULD YOU BE?

FEAR FACT: FOR "DEFILING" THE SACRED PREPARATION CHAMBER OF PRIESTESS KHALA, UNCLE BEN, GABE, AND SARI WERE ALMOST BOILED ALIVE IN MOLTEN TAR!

ATIONS! You've trapped all these creatures on paper! Look at your earlier drawings. Do you see an improvement? Practice will continually improve your skills and you will never have to fear picking up a pencil again! *WAIT!* There it is . . . that scratching noise . . . and is that howling? Better get out the pencil and paper again. These nights alone in your room are enough to give you . . .